**Zoë Tucker** is passionate about picture books. Working as an art director and designer, she has the opportunity to work with authors, artists, and publishers from all over the world. Zoë lives and works on the south coast of England with her husband, Adam, and a cat called Murray. She is the author of many children's books, including *Greta and the Giants* (Frances Lincoln Children's Books) and *Ada and the Number-Crunching Machine* (NorthSouth Books).

For Matt, with love.–Z.T.

**Julianna Swaney** illustrates children's books for a living and couldn't feel luckier to have such an amazing job. She is the illustrator of the #1 *New York Times* bestselling *We Are the Gardeners* by Joanna Gaines and several other picture books. Julianna lives with her partner in a 1911 craftsman bungalow in Portland, Oregon, and loves reading nineteenth-century literature written by women. This is her first book for NorthSouth. Visit her at JuliannaSwaney.com.

**Climate neutral**
Print product
ClimatePartner.com/17658-2110-1001

Text copyright © 2022 by Zoë Tucker.
Illustrations copyright © 2022 by Julianna Swaney.

First published in Switzerland under the title *Ein Garten für uns.*
English text copyright © 2022 by NorthSouth Books, Inc., New York 10016.

First published in the United States, Great Britain, Canada, Australia, and New Zealand in 2022 by NorthSouth Books, Inc., an imprint of NordSüd Verlag AG, CH-8050 Zürich, Switzerland.

Distributed in the United States by NorthSouth Books, Inc., New York 10016.
Library of Congress Cataloging-in-Publication Data is available.

ISBN: 978-0-7358-4484-1 (trade edition)
1 3 5 7 9 • 10 8 6 4 2

Printed in Latvia, by Livonia Print, Riga
www.northsouth.com

# The Garden We Share

by Zoë Tucker · illustrated by Julianna Swaney

**North South**

On a bright spring morning
as the sun peeps shyly through the trees
we step out into the garden.

I hold the seeds tightly in my hand,
each little dot full of hope and promise.

We dig into the earth, burrowing down to hide our treasure.
Carefully, gently, we sow the seeds.

We scatter them on the ground like stars in the sky and quickly cover them with a blanket of sweet soil.

We wait....

The cool air turns to a warm breeze,
and the sun shines down to feed our souls.
And our garden.

Tiny shoots emerge like magic,
reaching, and growing, toward the light.
We whisper stories to each one,
sharing our hopes and dreams.

The rain falls, and a rainbow appears.

Petals of every shape and size burst into life,
and before long our garden is a riot of color.

Tiny red tomatoes hang with green sugar snap peas,
all jumbled together in a jungle of leaves.

Bright yellow zucchini and zingy orange pumpkins jostle on the ground, and all around us the sweet smell of basil and lavender fills the air.

We lie on a blanket in the grass and
listen to the gentle hum of the honeybee
as she drifts in …
and out
of the blooms.

The days grow long
and hazy.

As the sun
dips low to the ground,
we gather our treasure.
Snipping and picking, collecting and saving,
our arms full of gifts for our friends.

We gather together and
share stories late into the night.

And when the autumn light glows golden,
the seeds drop and we collect them,
wrapping each one like a secret note.

Petals fall, and colors fade—and you are gone.

The seeds I hold in my hand remind me of you.
And I am lost in thought. How can such tiny dots
hold such big memories?

The cold air of winter rushes in,
and the sun does not shine.

But on a bright spring morning
as the sun peeps shyly
through the trees,
I think of you.

I dig....

I sow....

I wait.

And as the morning air
warms my heart,
little shoots emerge like magic.
And you are with me again.

Zucchini

Calendula

Pumpkin

Carrot

Peas

Nasturtium

SUNFLOWER

Beans

Radish

Hock

Zinnia

Tomato

Poppy

lettuce

Beet
Root

CHARD

Echinacea